The Dingles

by Helen Levchuk

Illustrated by
John Bianchi

A Groundwood Book

Douglas & McIntyre
Vancouver • Toronto

For Gypsy, Pippin & Cia,
my dearest and most amusing friends.

H.L.

To Marg.

J.B.

Doris Dingle had three cats and she loved them with all her heart.

Donna, a snobby Siamese, spent most of the time sorting through her collection of bird feathers.

DeeDee preferred to tap Doris Dingle's cheek with her paw until Doris opened her mouth so wide that DeeDee could count her fillings. She also liked to check up Doris Dingle's nose to see what made it whistle.

Dayoh was just an all-round good guy who was digging a hole to China. When Doris called him she would yell, "*Day-oh, Day-day, Day-day, Day-oh*," and he would come bouncing, bopping and handspringing.

Every day was a wonderful day for the Dingles. But their favourite time was breakfast. After eating they would drink catmint tea in the sunshine, then go about their business in the backyard.

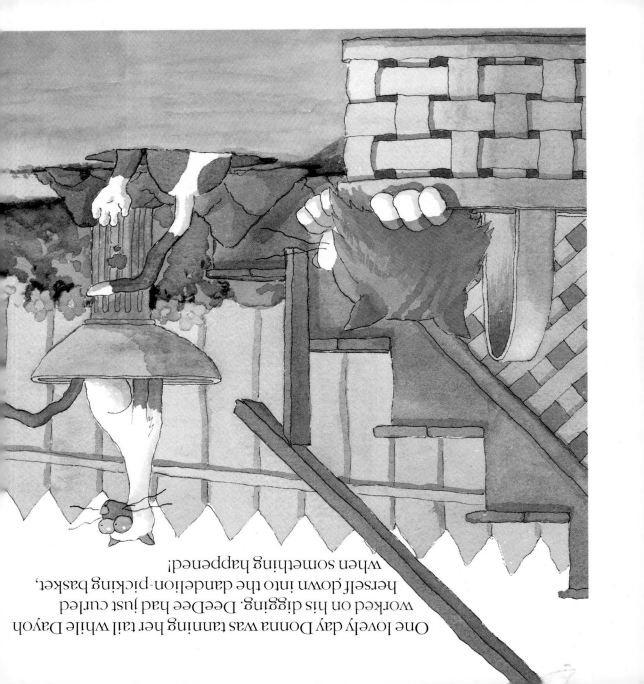

One lovely day Donna was tanning her tail while DayoH worked on his digging, DeeDee had just curled herself down into the dandelion-picking basket, when something happened!

It started out with a little breeze that blew away a few feathers.
Then came a wind that tipped over a big bag of peat moss.
A huge whoosh blew Doris Dingle's skirt right over her head.

Doris looked up and saw a little poodle dog-paddling across the sky. Then Mr. Gonzo's union suit blew by like a big red kite

with a clothesline tail—then his patio chairs and all the plastic
gnomes, flamingos and whirly-gigs.

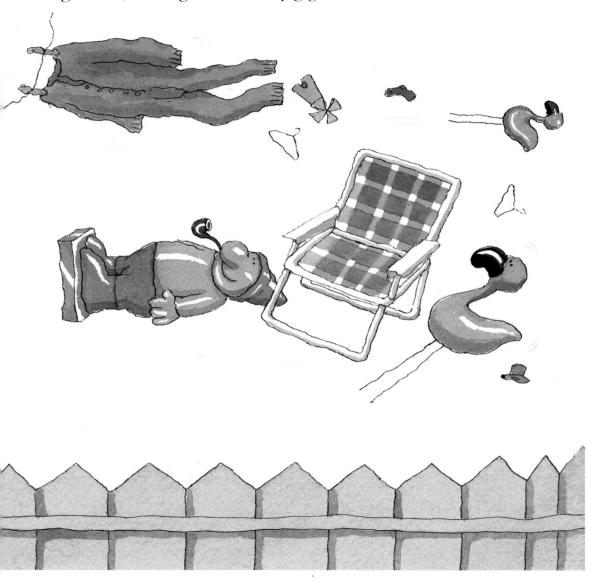

"We're going to be blown to Timbuctoo," screeched Doris, and sure enough, DeeDee came flying right by her and landed flat against the fence, spread out like a maple leaf.

Then Donna and Dayoh and flowerpots, garbage pails, lawn chairs and garden hoses dumped into a big rubble pile.

But even though Doris was very scared, she made a plan. Lifting her big apron, she tore the bottom into three long strips.

She tied one around each of the cats, then knotted all three to the waistband of her apron.

"Onward to the patio doors," Doris shouted, and they were off with their bellies to the ground—as flat as bearskin mats.

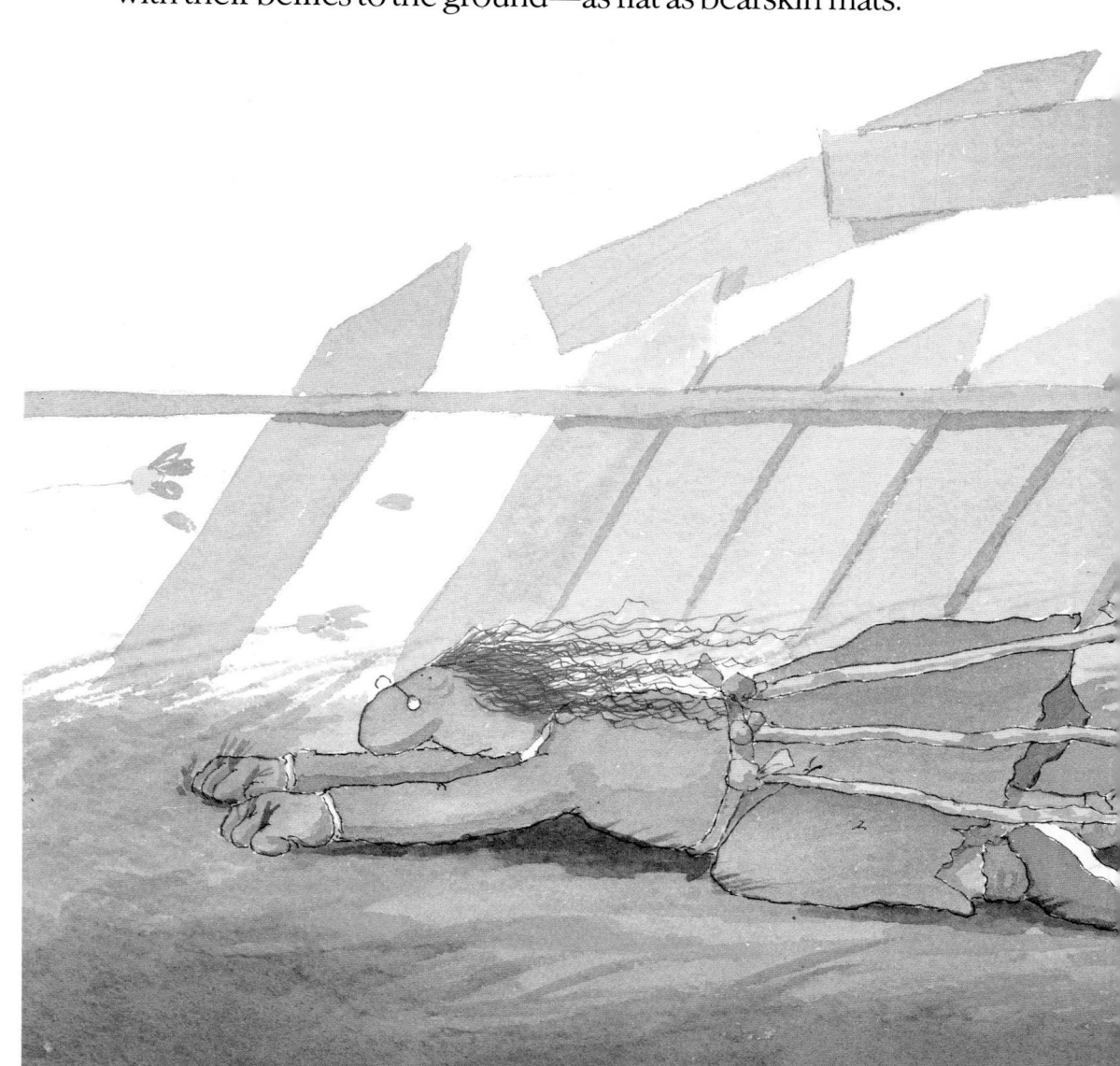

They clung to the ground and inched toward the doors. Donna got all twisted in her cord and the others dragged her along while she said her best prayers.

The sky turned black. Rain poured down. Then, lightning struck the fence post and shot the Dingles like missiles right through the doors and into the house.

The first thing they did was have a nice bath.

While the storm flashed and crashed outdoors Donna, DeeDee and Dayoh sat in a circle on the rug and had warm milk and honey with butter on top. Doris had a little catmint cordial to settle her nerves.

That night Doris, Donna, DeeDee
and Dayoh crawled into
Doris Dingle's feather bed. Two
minutes after Doris turned out
the light they were *zzzzzzzzzzzzzz*ing,
as the rain pitty-patted on the roof.
Everything was just as it should be.

A Groundwood Book
Douglas & McIntyre
585 Bloor Street West
Toronto, Ontario M6G 1K5

Third printing 1992

Canadian Cataloguing in Publication Data

Levchuk, Helen.
    The Dingles

ISBN 0-88899-044-8

I. Bianchi, John. II. Title.

PS8573.E94D56 1985   jC813'.54   C85-098901-9
PZ7.L48Di 1985